YOU SHOULD N

HEROES

A DCI Tallis: Celebrity Crimewave
novel, plus a short story

Gina Gallant

Do not put your trust in idols or make metal images of gods for yourselves

Leviticus 19:4, New Living Translation

I don't wanna grow up

There's too much contradiction

"Friction" by Tom Verlaine, from the Television album *Marquee Moon*

1

1972

Eric Tallis is excited, in that mid-teenage sort of way that most of us grow out of. Not for once the usual rampant male hormones, unless it's to do with the way they have an impact upon your cultural awareness. No, the fact is that he's got a highly prized ticket to see Jim Hellfire and his band at the Free Trade Hall, supported by...who was it now? Some second division band who've just been signed by Polydor, maybe make an album or two before being ditched by the company for not shifting the units at the required level, back to the day jobs...Eric and most of his fellow audience members will listen politely but not with too much enthusiasm because we all know whom they *really* came to see, that's why they're all dressed in woolly hats in homage to their idol, alongside the

Eric's mum has insisted he washes behind his ears before the event. "Who knows, you might meet a nice girl there," she says like she does every time he goes out by himself, which isn't all that often to be honest. He replies with a barely audible sneer, because girls are not the reason for going. Girls will be there, as the Jim Hellfire Band have gone some way to blurring the gender divide among fans in the style of Beatles, Bowie and Bolan, but Eric isn't going to the Free Trade to pull – that's just an optional extra – he's going for the camaraderie, the funny smells and, above all, the music.

Jim Hellfire, real surname Hepplewhite, is by now practically rock royalty. From his grammar school beginnings in the Key Tones – wannabe Beatles, their name an in-joke among A level biology students – he was the only member to turn pro while the others retreated to their medical education and careers, getting some fame in the late sixties with groups like The Deltoids and the late lamented Treacle, psychedelia of the highest order, and infused with the blues influence that permeates the sound of the current eponymous outfit. It's still rock though, rock of the new decade, characterised by Jim's sometimes extravagant but always melodic and imaginative guitar solos. He's a passable singer too.

The band members Phil Franks (organ, piano), Stuart Lamotte (bass, backing vocals), Roy Terry (drums, percussion, backing vocals) and Graham Shaw (alto and tenor sax) all have crucial roles to play on stage, and although none of them are overly involved in the songwriting and arrangements, the overall buzz (as *NME* might have it) is positive, and it's less of an ego trip than similar rock bands of this time. Why, the members still talk to each other and sometimes go for a drink or play footie together! They all look a bit alike too, despite slight variations in facial hair, and that always helps. Even their star signs are vaguely compatible, should you be interested in such things.

Outside his music, Jim's major passion is his pet dog Earl, an affectionate if rumbustious brown Labrador named after an obscure blues guitarist/singer – what else?! – who has developed a cupboard love for the other band members, who always spoil him when they come round to visit.

Oh, and let's not forget the roadies! They play a crucial role too behind the scenes, and Jim in particular is especially kind and polite towards them. Again, this is something we don't always see.

Concern is growing for the whereabouts and safety of Mary Miles, a 12 year old girl who's been missing from her home in Manchester for three days. Her last known whereabouts were as a member of the audience at the Jim Hellfire Band gig at the Free Trade Hall.

In October, a new release album, *Live at the Free Trade Hall* by the Jim Hellfire Band, is released to near unanimous critical acclaim ("sublime and eclectic" – *NME*; "a seminal work" – *Melody Maker*). There is some controversy surrounding its release, what with the Mary Miles disappearance still unresolved, but as any record company executive will tell you, any controversy is good controversy. The record sells by the bucketload, and Jim in a fit of altruism decides he'd like to donate an undisclosed proportion of his personal proceeds to Mary's parents.

Eric Tallis is proud of his moment in rock'n'roll history. He's the one on the live album yelling out a request for "M-M-Marvellous", one of the JHB's most recognisable and popular tunes. This is enough to gain young Eric a fair amount of attention at school, even among the scruffy set as the track inches its way up the singles charts in the run-up to Christmas. Amongst his family too, Eric is enjoying some celebrity status – even his mother is impressed by his bravado. Okay, it's not quite on the same footing as the guy who shouted "Judas" at Bob Dylan at the same venue a few years back, but it's there for posterity.

"And he's normally so quiet" is the typical comment of those who know the lad best.

"I just caught up in the moment", says the lad when questioned about it, semi-apologetic and red-faced.

2

1984

Jim Hellfire takes his new dog, name of Bukka, for their daily walk in the grounds of the castle he bought in '73 with some of the money he'd raked in from the sales of the live album: behaviour you'd come to expect from a major league music legend in those days of extravagance while the rest of us were lighting candles and relying on battery-operated radios to cope with the power cuts.

Both are satisfied with this arrangement. There are plenty of bitches come visiting, never mind the ladies, to spoil the pair of them and maintain the lifestyle they always sought after.

Why, Jim has even experimented with marriage to a couple of them, not that either endured. The first was with a model, Seventies definition, who, worried that her days in the glamour industry were numbered at the age of 25, decided to re-launch herself as a bit of a singer/songwriter. An album, produced and effectively co-written by Jim Hellfire, and featuring the classic JHB line-up, was released and deleted in fairly short order. The marriage too was deleted with even greater haste, "irreconcilable differences".

The second was with a graphic artist who designed a JHB album cover – quite a nice one – while they were together, but wasn't invited to repeat the task after Jim's adultery put paid to their wedded bliss. So now, approaching 40, he's still the big kid, not wishing to make the same mistake more than twice. No children have ensued from the legal partnerships, nor to his knowledge from any of his many casual acquaintances, which comes as some relief.

Jim is still selling records, if not in the vast quantities of the previous decade. The purge of 1976/7 meant a distinct drop in critical support, the more economic guitar sound of the Pistols and Ramones being more in favour than elaborate extended solos. He's retained his fan base – there'll always be the diehards – but not his band, the albums and tours now featuring session musicians rather than permanent members.

Phil Franks left in a huff in 1981 after being told he'd now be required to play synthesiser. Ditto Roy Terry the following year in a rage against the drum machine, converting his established part-time hippy existence in Formentera into a full-time one, making a sort-of living painting landscapes and seascapes for the tourists. Graham Shaw had already gone in '76 to do session work and be there for his young family, though he's still on good terms with Jim, and turns up for album recordings when required. Only Stuart Lamotte has remained loyal, and prevented the JHB family tree from turning into King Crimson's.

There's a nice wooded area in the castle grounds, as there should be, and Jim tends to take Bukka round there rather than go anywhere too public. As also tends to be the case, he'll pause for a minute and gaze at some disturbed earth with a rather sad look in his eye. The dog, sensing the master's discomfort, will do the same.

Mr & Mrs Miles are still none the wiser as to the fate of their daughter. She'd be 24 now, maybe with her own career, maybe married with a kid like they were. Probably the former option, because that's what a lot of young women are doing nowadays, and Mary did have a bit of a gift for languages and was a dab hand with her Brother typewriter. Maybe a job on the European Community gravy train? It's probably academic, though – at least in the eyes of the law she's dead.

But even if a body did turn up, that might just be a relief to them. It's the not knowing. Yes, they accepted the charity of Jim Hellfire, never questioning the motives behind it – they weren't well-off people back in '72 anyway. But money's never adequate compensation for a life, is it?

Eric Tallis is now enjoying his new function as a role model for his young niece. Susan hadn't even been born the night he went to see Jim Hellfire play Manchester, but she's now with his help developing an affection for the music, impressed by the sound of the guitar and the irregular rhythms that he brings with him in his magical record shop bag when he comes round to visit. She keeps time to it with her ad hoc percussion instruments – wooden rulers, kitchen cutlery - as well as any professional drummer.

A pity, Eric thinks, that she's stuck with his boring elder brother for a father. With his staid musical tastes, Daddy isn't likely to provide any encouragement for her to develop her musical interest – Santa Claus isn't going to be bringing a drum kit down the chimney in the foreseeable future. He'll probably railroad her into some unexciting daily grind of a job to make sure all the bills are paid on time when that time comes.

But for now it's good to see that Susan is making some positive steps, in her own way. He'll keep providing the turntables and the LPs, those new CD thingummies are just a rip-off, a flash in the pan. She's bright, she'll learn – the radio might provide you with a bit of U2 and The Smiths at its own discretion amongst the usual rubbish, even on a good day some Van Halen and ZZ Top, but with your own turntable you're the boss. It's *your* music, it's *your* choice, man.

3

Present day

Heather Williamson walks hesitantly into the reception area of Celebrity Task Force, nervously looking around her and back outside again, as if to wonder whether it'd be safer not to do what she came here to do.

Eventually she summons up the courage to approach the front desk.

"I want to report a case of historical abuse", she says, addressing the desk itself rather than the person behind it. From her regular visits to her GP, she knows that such people are invariably idiots.

"Okay," says the receptionist, trying to sound as soft-voiced and sympathetic as she can, "I just need to take some basic details from you. The victim of this abuse, was it yourself?"

Heather nods.

"And the person responsible?"

"Is a celebrity, yes. His name, or should I say his stage name, is Jim Hellfire."

The receptionist doesn't react. She's only 23, 40 years younger than Heather, and such names as Jim's don't really register with that age group. She adopts the default position of asking Heather to take a seat and an officer will be along to see her shortly.

McManus listens attentively to Heather's story. She, along with her best friend Mary Miles, had been to a concert given by the rock star and his band at the Free Trade Hall in 1972.

4

1972

Heather Williamson calls at Mary Miles' home and waits for her friend to get ready. Mary's mum offers her a cup of tea while she's waiting, but Heather declines.

They go into town together on the 50 bus, upper deck, chatting their schoolgirl chatter in 70s style. They get off the bus at the stop before the Albert Square terminus, the one nearest the venue. Once their .tickets have been looked at and separated, they have to get past a row of hairy students to get to their seats.

Like everyone else, they enjoy the music.

When the concert's over, Mary announces that she's going to try and get some autographs, and asks Heather to wait around for her.

She does so, but after a while she gets impatient. If she has to hang about any longer, she'll have to get the night bus, and they charge double fares for that. She makes one final, cursory look round and decides she'd be better off going home by herself and sorting it out with Mary tomorrow.

She feels a hand on her shoulder.

"You looking for somebody?" asks a gruff male voice.

Three hours later she's on the double fare night bus, anticipating the row she's going to have with her parents. She doesn't know what's happened in those three hours, but there's £5 more in her bag than she thought she'd had. Maybe it might have been better to get a taxi? Well maybe, if you're thinking straight.

5

Present day

"Nobody took you seriously in those days if you made accusations like that", Heather tells McManus.

"I know", says the detective, knowing the culture and history.

"And I know he was inside me!" She pauses. "Back then I was really naive, and I think he sensed that. I didn't know what was going on, what was...happening to me."

"You shouldn't have been expected to."

Superintendent Jarvis beckons DCI Tallis into his office on her return from a diversity and inclusion conference, whose contents went in one ear and out the other, the following day. He has what turns out to be startling news for her.

"You *what*?" she says in disbelief.

"One of your rock'n'roll heroes then?"

"And then some."

"Bit before your time though?"

"Yeah, I suppose, but I've got a stronger connection than that. My Uncle Eric was on one of his records."

"What?" Jarvis seems interested. "Was he a member of the band then?"

Sue explains the true story, note for note.

"That'd be the same concert where this incident is alleged to have happened", Jarvis adds, more prosaically. "Tell me, do you know anything about the Mary Miles case? Again, before your time but..."

"Vaguely. Girl that disappeared, never found, no body found either."

"Good. Well it turns out that Mary went to the concert with Heather, the woman who's making the complaint now, left her to do some autograph hunting and hasn't been seen since. Parents died not knowing what'd happened to her, Lord knows what that must've been like for them."

"So it's all part of the same set-up?"

"It's a possibility, and we're working on it."

"Then why take Mary and leave Heather behind?"

"That's one of the things we're trying to work on. Perhaps Mary was more his type, you know how paedos' minds work."

"I still can't get my head round this", Sue admits. "There've never been any allegations of abuse made against Jim Hellfire before, have there?"

"Not to our awareness."

"Or members of his group at the time?"

Jarvis shakes his head.

"So we're expected to go hammer and tongs against a 78-year-old man on one person's say-so?"

"I knew you'd say that sooner or later. You seem to have forgotten about Mary Miles already."

"Well-l-l...she could've just been wandering the streets of central Manchester after midnight, and any old nonce could've got a hold of her."

"It's a big coincidence if it happened that way", says Jarvis.

"Yeah, I suppose..."

"Look, you've got every right not to take everything at face value at this stage. But McManus is establishing a good rapport with Heather, and I don't want you going muscling in, demanding to know why it took her so long to make a complaint."

Sue's angered. "What do you take me for, sir? I know why it took her so long: (a) she was in denial to herself about it, (b) she probably reckoned she'd be making trouble for her parents, and (c) how do you think the police of Manchester in the seventies and for thirty years after are going to react to a story like that? They'd laugh her out of the station like they did with Savile's victims. Bootle Street rolled up trouser brigade!"

"Okay, you've said your bit, now calm down. Most of Savile's offences were in Yorkshire, for one thing."

Sue exhales, but Jarvis goes on before she's got chance to interrupt.

"And for another, Heather Williamson isn't one of those old biddies you normally take such an instant dislike to. She's actually quite introverted, timid even."

"Yes, your typical abuse victim", says Sue a little cynically. "Before you ask, there could be any number of reasons why she turned out like that."

"I know that! But we have to tread carefully. I'm not getting the press involved with this yet – I don't want a load of tabloid hacks starting a witch hunt without good reason. Meanwhile...I suppose you've got a slight conflict of interest here, but no worse than what you normally have. I'd like you to make use of your...well let's call it insider knowledge."

"In the interests of justice", Sue says, finally cracking a trace of a smile. "And I think I know a man who can help."

6

"It's been a long time", says Uncle Eric.

"Since you did the rewiring, wasn't it?" Mother offers helpfully. We're in her front room, getting ready for a nice afternoon tea by common consent, although Sue's arrangements for it were a little last-minute. Eric didn't need much persuasion to attend, especially with Sue's chauffeuring service being added as an extra bonus, although Mum needed a bit more convincing: "There's a new craft baker opened up, getting rave reviews on Trustpilot, the Super recommends it." Free-from sandwiches and cakes on the menu no less, so everybody's happy.

Sue unpacks the food, which she stopped off to get on the journey with Eric, in the kitchen while the two in-laws try their best to catch up.

"Well, if you ever get a second-hand microwave that needs PAT testing..." says Uncle, clinging to the DIY theme. He's always been a little tongue-tied in the company of Sue's mother, and relative old age seems to have done little to dissipate this. When they were younger, he fancied her a bit but never let on, her being a little bit older for one thing, and her being his boring but heavier brother's chosen partner for another.

He'd got good with electrics in his younger days, concluding that if you can't be in a band, the next best thing was to generate some electricity of your own. He didn't like it when they bowed to pressure and started selling items with the plug already on, because he made a decent sideline from people who were scared witless of electrocuting themselves if they made a mess of the wiring.

It's good to have a passion or two, he always thought. Lack of passion was what killed his brother in the end, he maintains. He's already outlived him in terms of miles on the clock. Eric's career was one thing, but ultimately his main obsession was still – *is* still – the music. That of course was Sue's reason for organising this mini family conference.

She brings in the fare with all the finesse of the staff she remembered from the case at Lucy's Tea Room a couple of years back. Nothing ends up on the floor, which is quite an achievement.

"I hope you like Susan's choices of refreshment, Eric," says Mother without any trace of irony, "she has to have gluten free these days."

"*Dairy* free, Mother", Sue corrects, "and every bit as good as the so-called real thing." Mum never had any training in nutrition, just in cooking. She'd never have got a job at Pret à Manger.

Mother ignores her. "Well don't be shy, tuck in", she gestures, mainly at Eric.

And a good tea is had by all.

Sue waits until everyone has had sufficient to eliminate the thought of any evening meal, even sleepwalking her way through all the small talk and gossip, before disclosing her true purpose.

"Eric...I've just been listening a bit to *Live at the Free Trade Hall* again, and I'm interested in hearing your memories about it."

"Oh, if you're going to talk about music I might as well go and do the washing up", says Mother. Eric grins, Sue doesn't, and Mother collects up the plates and leaves them to wonder whether or not she's being serious.

Eric chuckles when he thinks she's out of earshot. "Demis Roussos, Brotherhood of Man, Paper Lace – that was the extent of your mother's 1970s."

Sue smiles. But they've got serious things of their own to consider. "The live album?"

"Oh yeah, forgive me. Great album, up there with *Live and Dangerous* and *Live at Leeds*, I'll never forget that night."

"No, well it's there for posterity, along with your personal contribution. But I'm wondering, could you put a little background information to it?"

"Why, are you thinking of going on *Mastermind* with it?"

She laughs. "I might."

"Yeah well, if you do as well with it as you could, you'd probably only need to get ten of the general knowledge questions right."

"That's what I'm worried about!"

"Well try me, I'll do my best."

"For instance, I read on Wikipedia that it was the JHB's final concert of the '72 tour. Is that right?"

"Correct."

"Do you know why it was Manchester not London? Bands usually finished by doing one of the big London arenas, didn't they?"

"That's true, and probably still is. But I think I know why Jim did it that way. Firstly, he's got family connections to the Manchester area, spent his childhood...ooh, somewhere up Oldham Road I think. Secondly, and I got this from music press interviews he did at the time, he never really liked London. Always associated it with the musical parasites – managers, agents, fashionable journalists, hangers-on..."

"They must've toured the country in a funny way", Sue suggests.

Eric laughs. "Quite a few bands did in those days. A lot of 'em were too drugged up and pissed to care. But no, I think they *started* in London, went to Bristol and Cardiff, then zig-zagged back to do the east side – Leicester, Sheffield, Newcastle, couple of places in Scotland – then down to Liverpool and then Manchester."

"Okay, that's fine, that's good to know." If Jim and his cronies knew that they were demob happy, it might affect their behaviour. "Do you remember much about the audience?"

Crucial question in Sue's eyes, but not a crucial answer in Eric's: "Not much really, especially after all this time. Usual rock crowd I'd say – denims, long hair, joss sticks."

"Male? Female? Young? Older?"

"Probably about two thirds male, sixth formers and students mainly, some sixties renegades, a few teenyboppers, which surprised me a little, but then he was in the singles charts a few times, so –"

"Did you have anything to do with any other people in the audience?"

"Oh, a bit of chat with the guy in the next seat while we were waiting, just about the band, music tastes in general, you know the score. There was the usual commotion afterwards, but I didn't get involved. I was tired, wanted to get home – could've followed 'em to a pub and got an illegal pint, but as it happens I didn't."

"And did you notice anything unusual happening among the crowd?"

"Now you're sounding like a copper!" Eric pauses for thought. "Is this to do with that missing girl?"

7

Eric Tallis never married. That fact about a man in his sixties might have generated idle rumours and suspicions half a century ago, but...aren't we supposed to be more "enlightened" now?

He had a long-term relationship with a woman called Sally, whom Sue remembers was around quite a bit during her childhood. Then one day she up and left, for reasons best known to herself. She's known to have got hitched to another bloke a year later, so evidently she was more comfortable with the idea of wedded bliss than Eric was. No more was heard about her, no mention made.

Sue pores over Eric's visits to her parents' house all those years ago. There were times when he was alone with her, certainly, but that was when he was giving her her musical education, and there was nothing else to it – was there?

Of course not. If there was, she'd know about it, wouldn't she?

Oh, why am I so suspicious, she thought. He was a fifteen year old boy only interested in fifteen year old girls, maybe slightly older but not a second younger. How would he have the motive, means and opportunity to rape one girl whom he didn't know from Adam, arrange the disappearance of another, and still be home before the pubs shut? Why would he want to? And as for his healthy long term memory about the concert, wouldn't he be expected to remember "that missing girl", since the two events were so bound up together?

Susan Tallis never married either, for that matter, and there's nothing suspicious about that. Like Eric, she's experienced the odd near miss but, also like him, she could just say she was being careful in that aspect of her life.

Heather Williamson has also remained single, we learn at the case conference. And she's the supposed victim.

Jack McManus has succeeded in gaining her confidence. He's like that, he knows how to press the right buttons, how to listen and how to let your conversation partner know you're listening, and – most important of all – when to shut up.

He now effectively has Heather's life story from the crime onwards. She knew something wasn't quite right, but she didn't have the words or the confidence to express it. She lost all interest in pop and rock music in general, and the Hellfire Band in particular, with immediate effect. She couldn't bear to have their records in her room, selling her copies of their 33s and stand-alone 45s, all in immaculate condition, to a school friend for a couple of quid.

She got five O levels, stayed on for sixth form but could only scrape a couple of A levels, but that was enough to get her a job at a bank and spare her the indignity of being one of Thatcher's

Three Million. She performed to the best of her ability in the post, gaining the occasional promotion and concomitant salary increase, until she reached her pinnacle of deputy manager of the Stockport branch.

As befitted her position, she saved prudently and treated herself occasionally, mainly to solo holidays. She visited each continent at least once. She buried her parents when the time eventually came, but didn't see this as licence to do anything wildly different, not even with the small inheritances they'd both left her. She dallied with men, and the occasional woman, during her breaks abroad, but never considered anything permanent.

Emboldened by those who had made successful allegations against celebrities, she finally gathered up the courage to tell of her own experience. Her physical and mental health, never a hundred per cent, has been declining yet more in late middle age. This could be her last chance to do something meaningful, *really* meaningful.

She never forgot Mary.

"And she's sticking by her story?" asks Sue.

"Word for word", McManus replies.

"Then I think it's time for us to do a little home visiting, Jack. Don't forget your toothbrush."

8

James Hepplewhite celebrated his fiftieth anniversary as a castle freeholder in 2023. There's his birth name on the title deeds, look; an Englishman's home, indeed.

In the early days of his ownership, the building took on the appearance of a scene from a contemporary schlock horror film; this was partly to fit in with Jim Hellfire's own personality profile, partly on the advice of his manager that he could easily make a second income hiring the place out to movie production companies, giving him the chance to hobnob and share a photo opportunities with Joan Collins or Peter Cushing or somebody.

The plan never came to fruition. Popular culture's schoolboy flirtation with the gothic and satanic soon went undercover, and as time went on, Jim's tastes got more conservative, and by the eighties the only regular visitors were dogs and groupies, in that order.

There's a lot of that drink- and drug-related behaviour that 78-year-old James now regrets. It had damaged himself in certain ways, and had a negative effect on many of those around him. In his old age, he's tried to repent, and it looks like he's making a pretty good job of it. He started attending church five years ago, for the first time since childhood, and although Covid tried its best to interrupt that, he's back in full swing now, doing his Psalm readings with the same gusto he once applied to classic rock lyrics. The dogs and their exercise regimes became too much of a burden shortly before the new millennium, but he replaced that pastime by developing an interest in ornithology. You could see or hear him on TV nature programmes or the occasional Radio 4 *Tweet of the Day*; well, if it's good enough for Bill Oddie...

"We all sell out eventually", he once joked on X.

He still performs his music, but much less frequently. The live album got its golden anniversary rehash in 2022 on expensive vinyl with all the customary specialist fanfare, which enabled

Jim and his surviving comrades in arms to do a few targeted gigs, and spend the winter of 2022-3 recording an album of blues standards that was generally well received and sold a respectable number of units by today's standards. Graham Shaw, and even Roy Terry, still on loan from Formentera – how does he do it - were involved in the recording and accompanying small-venue tour. There was talk of an old-timers' package tour with a few other hoary rock survivors, but terms couldn't be agreed.

As with most groups of that era, the classic line-up didn't all make it to the present day. Phil Franks died of prostate cancer in 2011, there was a good fundraising gig held in his honour, and Jim hatas proud to perform a few tracks from the '72 live album in memoriam. Stuart Lamotte passed in 2020, an early victim of coronavirus, and the tributes were a little more muted.

But overall, life's been kind to James Hepplewhite himself, and he's grateful for it.

Some things never change though, for example cops at the door.

"Mr Hepplewhite? Mr James Hepplewhite?" It's left to McManus to perform the introductions and vaguely explain the purpose of the visit. Sue, still not sure about exactly how she should behave here, produces her warrant card on cue and enters the building at the owner's reluctant invitation.

"I have to tell you that a serious accusation of a sexual nature has been made against you", says McManus when they're all uncomfortably seated.

"What?!" exclaims the rock star, a reaction which, though common, tells nobody anything.

McManus outlines the complaint. He's the one who's had the most contact with the victim, after all.

"I don't believe this. Fifty years ago? And I'm supposed to supply you with an alibi?"

"You could try."

Sue senses the opportunity to nose in. "It was the night you recorded your live album in Manchester."

"Oh, you've done your research have you?" Jim says with enough irony. This isn't going to be easy.

"I have good sources", Sue replies.

"Have you got any recollection of what you did after the concert was over?" asks McManus.

"Not 100%. Last gig of a tour, I'd normally just get the hell out as soon as possible. I'd be tired, and I was never one for hobnobbing at any excuse. So yeah, I'd just get back to the hotel and let the other guys and the roadies have some fun on their own."

"I see", says McManus. He doesn't really.

"Look, this...complainant of yours, she's absolutely sure it was me, is she?"

"That's what she's been telling us", says McManus. "She gave a good description of you that fits in with the archive photos of you that we've accessed."

"And I suppose you've got DNA evidence to back this up?"

Touchê. "That sort of evidence, as you probably know, wasn't available in those days."

"So what *have* you got? You've got one person, half a century on with half a century of false memories planted in her head by some quack shrink or other. Let me give you my side. First, even in those days I wouldn't think of doing anything like that. Yes, I know there were people in rock music of the time who thought they were empowering the kids by having sex with them, but I was never a member of that club. Second, and this is to do with this description that you're so keen on, a lot of guys looked like me. A lot of fans tried their best to look like me! I bet half the audience at the Free Trade looked like me – at the time it was a good way to pull the birds. Plus one or two of the road crew, even Roy, my drummer at the time, people often thought we were brothers."

"We're also re-opening investigations into the murder of Mary Miles" is Sue's counter. It sounds quite feeble in the circumstances.

"What, her than went missing?"

Sue nods.

"So are you saying that I'm responsible for that as well? By all accounts I had a very busy night."

"The two girls involved were connected to each other."

"I'm sorry, is that supposed to impress me?"

"It's enough to suggest there's also a connection between the things that happened to them."

"You never found the girl's body, did you?"

"After this amount of time, we've every reason to suspect she was unlawfully killed."

McManus intervenes. "A property like this would be a suitable place to hide a body."

"You've been watching too many films, officer", says Jim. "For your information, I didn't buy the place till a year after I did that gig. Are you saying I killed her, kept the body in a freezer for a year before deciding it'd be better off in my secret chamber?! Do you know how ridiculous you sound?"

Sue hesitates before announcing: "We'd like you to come back to Manchester with us."

"Am I under arrest?"

"If you're innocent, you've got nothing to fear."

"I need to contact my brief. I'm not having one of your pound shop lawyers."

"Good work," says Jarvis over the phone. "Now that you've made the arrest, the time's right for us to go public over this. With any luck, a few more victims might find the courage."

9

You'd have a job mistaking Roy Terry for James Hepplewhite these days. Roy's about a stone heavier than his "brother", with a bit less hair though he's making a vain attempt to convince people otherwise with his rattail.

Like Jim, he's trying to make it look like he's living the good life. While the boss has his birdwatching and his years of dog walking to stir his passions and keep him healthy, the drummer's got ingredients of his own: a healthy Mediterranean diet for one thing, and – advantage Roy – a long-term partner he still loves. Not to mention his artist's impressions of houses iced in whitewash guarding pale shore lines. And he can still keep time, the old-fashioned way.

But the music was never going to be enough on its own. The industry has a depressing list of people who "lived for the music" and ended up dead at the age of 27. And now here Roy is, almost three times that age, and showing no signs of packing it in just yet.

He doesn't remember much about that night in Manchester in '72, post-gig: signing a few autographs maybe, but then he did that most concert nights.

Graham Shaw, the other surviving JHB member, also looks out to sea from where he lives, but it's the slightly more modest setting of the Norfolk coast. Like everyone, he's got his home studio, but he's within reasonable travelling distance of the London establishments should a seasoned saxophonist be required. After feeling he was the overlooked member of the JHB, especially among producers who treated anything beyond basic guitar/bass/drums as mere sweeteners, he's pleasantly surprised that his name's still in the hat, frequently with artists young enough to be his grandchildren; obviously their advisors have some appreciation of rock history, even if the artists themselves don't.

Speaking of grandchildren, Graham has quite a few now, mostly in young adulthood. The kids left home long ago and dutifully began breeding, although the new generation isn't in quite such a hurry, and he might have to wait around a few years before he gets the honour of being a great-grandfather.

But Graham makes sure that the clan are gathered together each Christmas, and it's the complete middle-class idyll.

He doesn't muse too much about the reasons for his personal and professional longevity. Put it down to the multivitamins if you like.

He doesn't remember much about that night in Manchester in '72, post-gig: signing a few autographs maybe, but then he did that most concert nights.

10

Once all the cranks and attention-seekers had been eliminated, the number of legitimate accusations against Jim Hellfire, minus Heather Williamson's, amounted to precisely zero.

"All we've got against him is a rock star attitude," Sue tells Jarvis, "and even that's excusable in the circumstances."

"That's the trouble with those mind-enhancing drugs", says the superintendent. "Nobody knew or cared what they were doing."

"And after fifty years, they're not going to. And now you've got dementia coming into the picture as well. He's all lawyered up now, won't tell us any more than he has done already. We're just not gonna have a case."

"Come to my office this afternoon about 2. I might have a surprise for you."

"Sue, let me introduce you to former Detective Chief Inspector Peter Craig, Senior Investigating Officer on the Mary Miles disappearance."

Sat in a chair in Jarvis' office, at 2pm precisely, is a man in his nineties. White-haired, wrinkly to be sure, carrying a bit less weight than he probably did back then, well kempt and smartly dressed including a tie that he'd probably wear to a hospital appointment as well, he stands up to greet her with a firm handshake that belies his weight loss.

"Pleased to meet you", she says all businesslike and borderline sincere.

"Yes, likewise", Craig grunts. "I see there've been plenty of changes to the set-up since I was around."

Jarvis pours the tea and hands his guests their drinks. He's even got biscuits, "dairy free shortbreads", in anticipation of a thoroughly civilised discussion between the representatives of the different eras.

"In my day," Craig says, pursuing his theme, "it was a middle-aged mother of four with a tea trolley and whatever strained rubbish she could find to put on it. And we were supposed to be grateful she wasn't on some trade union work to rule."

Jarvis laughs. "Well, at least some things are looking up."

Sue doesn't laugh. If it's going to be an afternoon of small talk reminiscences, she thinks, it's going to be a wasted one.

"Course we never had such a thing as a special unit for celebrities", the older man continues. "We treated 'em all the same, villains or victims, whether they were on the telly or not."

Sue won't let that one pass. "Oh, I think there were a few people who were on the telly whose crimes got overlooked."

Craig's getting agitated. "Such as?"

Sue scoffs. "Do I really need to give you the names?"

Jarvis senses that things aren't going entirely according to plan, and tries to neutralise the situation. "I asked Peter here because I thought he could give us some insight into the original investigation, and maybe save us from repeating ourselves."

"Once I heard things were rolling again," says Craig, "I had to come along and offer my services. Course I know time's moved on, some of the original cast are no longer with us, but my memory's still good and I won't have anybody saying otherwise."

"So what did you actually *do*?" asks Sue, a little impatient.

"Me and my team got to work on the longhairs – the group, their entourage, the few members of the audience who volunteered to give us information. Couldn't get an ounce of sense out of most of them – junkies and wasters, the *lot* of 'em...so we had no immediate leads. We put out appeals, "have you seen this girl" sort of thing, and of course then we're plagued with timewasters, as I daresay you would be now. We kept the investigation live for as long as we could, but inevitably time has its effect, other cases demand greater priority and, well..."

"You got nowhere?" says Sue.

"No, we didn't get nowhere. I had some strong suspicions, just not enough to charge anybody with."

"So who *would* you have charged? James Hepplewhite?"

"He was as shady as anybody. Grubby little devil, but as rich as the Pope. I'm not the least bit surprised that you're looking at him for rape. Mind you, the people around him were all lickspittles, could easily have been covering up for each other."

"So you weren't exactly sympathetic to the counterculture?"

Craig grins, as if to mock the question. "I'll tell you a bit about this 'counterculture', shall I? Hairy louts on stage, calling the police pigs, shouting out pro-IRA slogans, more or less encouraging their audiences to go on demos and attack us. And of course that's what happens. We get spat at, punched, kicked, verbally abused."

"Maybe some of your lot *acted* like pigs."

For Craig, that's the red rag. "How dare you!"

"Come on, we all know how free you could be with your truncheons in those days. Demonstrators often came off worse against mounted police covering up their ID numbers."

"Whose side are you on, miss?"

"The side of justice, thank you for asking. And please don't call me 'miss'. You didn't outrank me then, and you certainly don't outrank me now."

Jarvis, silent for a considerable time, now feels the need to play the umpire again. "Look, can we calm down, for heaven's sake?"

Craig takes a few deep breaths. "Look," he says, looking at Sue, "what you're describing didn't happen on my watch."

"You're 100% sure about that? Not one bad apple? In the Seventies?!"

Craig pauses to reflect, then reluctantly spills out: "Alan Rogers."

"Who?" asks Jarvis.

"Alan Rogers, DC on my team. In his twenties, family man already but something not quite right about him. Nothing concrete against him, but I dunno, call it a gut feeling."

"And of course there wasn't enough evidence", says Sue tautologically.

"What happened to him?" asks Jarvis.

Craig tries to recall. He takes a deep breath. "Left the force in '74, we assumed down to frustration at not getting a promotion."

"It happens", sighs Jarvis.

"Got a job as a swimming instructor."

"What, like at a health club?"

"Oh God no, no – at those council baths that should've been pulled down fifty years before they actually were."

Sue's ears prick up. "So he was working with school parties?"

"Yes, I expect so."

"Well that was a licence to commit child abuse in those days! Do a deal with the pervy teacher who's accompanying them to the baths on the bus..."

"He got the MBE in 2007 for his thirty plus years of service in helping people learn to swim."

"Well, that means nothing", says Sue. "He wouldn't have been the first nonce to get an award like that."

"He sounds like someone we could do with speaking with", says Jarvis. "Any idea where we can find him?"

Craig grins. "Try Southern Cemetery. He had a heart attack the year after he got his gong. Body and conscience couldn't take it, I expect."

Craig takes Jarvis aside before he takes his leave.

"Keep on at Hepplewhite about the drugs angle. You're bound to get him confused about that. And watch *her* – she'll be after your job before you know it, and with all this political correctness she'll have it."

Jarvis shakes his hand. "Goodbye Peter, and thanks for your input."

Sue's still sat down. When Craig's out of the way, Jarvis closes the door. Debriefing is one of his fortes, but it wasn't expected for this occasion.

"Old as he is, there were times when I could've taken a swing at him", she says.

"He'd probably have hit you back."

She smiles faintly. "Blame it on the generation gap."

He chuckles. "One of the occupational hazards of cold cases."

Sue changes the subject. "So you're not going to be giving me a black mark for insubordination?"

"Why should I? Like you said, he never outranked you."

"Except in his own mind."

11

They keep on at Hepplewhite about the drugs angle, but to no avail, and when the time comes they have to release him. He drives back to the castle with his legal representative.

The forensic team have had time to inspect Jim's home, but find nothing of interest, no traces, no secret passages, no fake panels. Jarvis orders them to concentrate now on the grounds, so Jim can have a good look at them out the window as he's ruminating.

He's not been charged, but the mud of the tabloids and the telly and the internet will stick. He won't be going to church this Sunday, because if he did 90% of the parish will be going (or staying) home. His radio tweets will be put on ice pending due process. As for his social media (formerly known as) tweets, they would be pointless and he'd be subject to the loss of xK followers no matter what – best avoid all the speculation and gossip, eh? Even the rock stations daren't play his music.

Meanwhile DCI Tallis is looking into the life of former Detective Constable Alan Rogers. There's not much to find: a Google search only reveals an archive *Manchester Evening News* page about him receiving his MBE. No police record of criminal activity, but she half expected that. Apparently no reports of his death either, so no blog posts evoking fond memories of overcoming the fear of the deep end thanks to Mr Rogers' expert tuition? Seems not.

The *MEN* report did give an address in Withington for Rogers, or at least the name of the road because it was legal to do that then, but even a more detailed search couldn't uncover any more than suburban respectability and poll tax paid on time.

It's a dry day, so Jim decides he'll have a stroll outside and keep the forensic investigators company. He won't taunt them too much, though; that'd only make him seem more guilty in their eyes/

"Don't go any further, sir", says the man in the white protective suit as Jim approaches the wooded area. "We don't want to risk contaminating evidence."

"Look," Jim replies, "any recent DNA you find in there will be mine anyway. 'I stick to a tree/and the tree it sticks to me'. I used those lines in a song once."

Which is true: the words form part of the lyrics of "M-M-Marvellous", the song that Eric Tallis was so keen to see performed at the Free Trade. The examiner, straight out of a third-tier university with a degree in forensic whatnot, is too professional to belittle Jim, so he gives his reply a positive slant so as not to appear too inhuman.

"You appear to have a good appreciation of the rudiments of forensic ecology, sir."

Jim is modest. "No more than anyone else. There are a lot of books available on the subject at the supermarket as much as in the academic library."

A colleague waves the white suit over to deeper in the woods, and he walks over, gesturing at Jim to stay put.

There is disturbance to the earth, something which would pass as a shallow grave. The team now devote all their energies to its uncovering. It's a hard job – this wasn't a recent piece of work – but their effort is rewarded when they dig deep enough to reveal the skeletal remains of – two dogs.

"Nice work", Jim says to White Suit shortly after. "I confess. But I think that's all you're gonna find. Any more discoveries and I reckon you're gonna have to have a few words about it with Oliver Cromwell."

12

1983

Earl has been a faithful companion during Jim's years of rock stardom, but old age and ill health have taken their toll, and on the vet's advice Jim agrees that it'd be cruel to prolong the animal's suffering.

After saying his goodbyes, Jim leaves the ensues. He takes the body home and gives it a private burial in the woods along with a toy that Earl was very partial to.

Some weeks later, a respectful length of time he feels, Jim acquires a new puppy from the animal shelter.

1999

Bukka too has a good innings, but sadly doesn't make it to the millennium. A different sort of personality to his previous pet, more caring and attentive, perhaps more introverted, less playful but not to the extent of being anti-social, and with radically different food preferences. Not "better" or "worse" than Earl – those terms are meaningless – but a healthy illustration of the variety of the canine world.

Jim remembers times when he'd taken Bukka for a walk in the woods, and they'd pause at the side of Earl's grave, and how the new dog seemed to sense his owner's sadness at these moments. It would be fitting, Jim decides, for them to share the same resting place.

Jim's well into his fifties now, and is starting to experience some of the discomforts of late middle age, human style. He thinks it'd be unfair to get a new dog now, fearing that by the time he reaches his three score years and ten – if he makes it that far – he won't be in a fit state to give the animal the exercise and attention they deserve. His years at the castle have given him an enhanced awareness and appreciation of the bird life of the area, and he thinks it would be a suitable, less physically demanding use of his time and resources to pursue ornithology as a hobby.

13

Present day

Eric Tallis is disappointed by the recent turn of events.

"I'm having to listen to my favourite record in secret, with headphones on, frightened that someone might report me for being inappropriate, like it's a Gary Glitter or Rolf Harris record", he complains.

The scene is Eric's flat, which he still boasts of, despite his advancing years, as being his "bachelor pad", Seventies style. Elements of that vintage still remain: haphazard "not gonna need that pan for a bit" washing up, lingering cooking smells – not bad ones, he's learned to be a decent chef when the mood takes him – pre-hipster paper posters that would have been free inserts with first edition LPs decorating the living room and bedroom walls.

Sue Tallis is paying him a social visit out of the goodness of her heart, with the aim of keeping him up to speed on developments that aren't too eyes-only. She wonders whether the visit was such a good idea after all.

"Look, I don't *want* him to be guilty," she blurts out, "but if he *is* guilty I'll make sure he gets what's coming to him."

"You still don't know if he's guilty?"

"We don't have enough evidence at the moment. There are other possible lines of enquiry."

"That's PR speak. The press seem to have made *their* minds up."

"You should know by now that the press twist things to suit their agenda. Then they get bored and find someone or something else to create a moral panic over."

"And by then the damage is done. 'No smoke without fire.'"

"I can't help what these tabloid scumbags write."

"But your lot can help what you feed 'em with in the first place. I suppose that makes you feel –"

"Uneasy." She finishes for him, "why, were you going to say 'powerful'?"

"I was, actually…well, doesn't it?"

"It doesn't make *me* feel powerful, no. I can't speak for the others."

At which point Sue, feeling that she's said all that's worth saying, terminates the discussion, reminding herself to tell Eric that mother would quite like to meet with him for a coffee if he's willing.

"I'll call her tomorrow", he promises.

14

10.30am. A plane arrives at Manchester Airport, Terminal 1, a few minutes ahead of schedule. After the usual clamour of getting the hand luggage out of the overhead compartments and waiting for the doors to open, its full load of passengers disembark and make their way into the terminal building. It's a dull day, but at least it's a dry one, cold enough for those among them who were unwise enough to come dressed for the temperature at their departure airport.

Among the group is a woman in her sixties, travelling alone. She makes her way to baggage reclaim unaccompanied, having dismissed the chance to indulge in small talk with someone she doesn't know from Adam.

Baggage reclaim takes its time, but once she's located her belongings, she trolleys them forward in haste, and mercifully customs and passport control have chosen this day to be kind to her.

The baggage is too heavy to take on public transport, however varied and cost-effective the three options to town may be, so she finds a taxi and asks the driver to take her to a medium- to high-end hotel in the city centre that she booked online a few days ago. She's comfortably off, but not made of money, so she feels this would be the right base for her for the immediate future.

It's lunchtime now, so she thinks she can at least check in at the hotel, and even if the servants haven't yet done their duties in her room, she can at least grab a sandwich and have an eye kept on her stuff until they're finished.

In the event, the previous occupant checked out immediately after breakfast, and there was plenty of time for the staff to tidy and spruce up the room, and she's allowed to take up residence without hindrance. She thanks the receptionist for being so obliging.

Once the clothes are on the right hangers, and the drawers full of her version of the essentials, she decides instead to do a bit of window shopping, and take her lunch at a café in town.

Apart from the food, she doesn't buy anything at the shops, but makes a mental note of a few department stores and one or two specialists for future reference – she'll be in town long enough to give her bank cards an airing.

Later in the afternoon, her attention is drawn to the passage of time and the main purpose of her city break. She takes a Metrolink tram – it's her maiden voyage on this service, even though it's been running for over thirty years, but she's read and heard encouraging reports about it – to Celebrity Task Force headquarters.

Once inside this building, she confidently strolls up to the front desk and asks to see a senior officer dealing with the Jim Hellfire investigation. She gives her name as Mary Miles.

15

It's not every day that someone walks into a police station and claims to be a person who's been presumed dead for fifty years, so naturally there's a bit of scepticism among the CTF detectives.

Jarvis, though he was preparing himself for going home for the night, doesn't want to miss out on an opportunity for a big moment, and co-opts the previously inactive DS Roche, who'd been spending as much time as he could get away with working on a report of his last assignment, a now-resolved minor case, to talk with "Mary".

"Can you prove it?" asks Jarvis. "Documents? Passport?"

She still has her passport on her – it'd be foolish to have left it in the hotel room – but she's reluctant.

Roche only permits a limited period of silence before becoming impatient. "Well?"

"I have my passport, but – "

"Then let's see it", says Jarvis.

She fumbles around in her bag, then hands the document over to the superintendent. It's a Spanish passport, which immediately raises eyebrows. Jarvis looks inside and then gives it to Roche who does likewise. They look at each other, bemused. It's Roche who voices concern first.

"The name on this is Maria Terry."

"That is the name that I'm now known as", she replies, trying not to sound too foreign. "A lot of women change their name at some point in their lives. You'll find my date of birth will match with any records you have – "

"Well, that *is* a 364-1 shot I admit. What do you think, sir, worth a tenner each way?" says Roche, smarmily.

"Your *place* of birth is given as San Francisco," Sir interjects, "Mary Miles was born and raised in Manchester. How do you explain that?"

"First, it's not the San Francisco you're probably thinking of. This is San Francisco, capital of Formentera in the Balearic Islands. Second, I had to make a new identity for myself."

"Why?" asks Roche.

"Personal reasons."

"That's not good enough", says Jarvis. "We're investigating some serious crimes here. If you *are* Mary Miles, you're going to have to do some explaining about what you've been doing since 1972, and why you chose not to let anybody know about it. If you're not Mary, then you're wasting our time and you're going to be in serious trouble for *that*."

"If I'm not Mary, I'm wasting my own time – and money."

"So?"

"When I saw those internet reports about Jim Hellfire being accused of child abuse and murder, I had to come along and say something." Her speech starts to become more hesitant. "I was being abused. But Jim Hellfire and his band had nothing to do with it."

"Okay," says Jarvis, "but you still haven't said why you've not said or done anything until now. You know your parents died without ever knowing what happened to you? That must've been hell for them."

She smiles slightly, but this isn't out of amusement. "Don't you understand? It was my parents I was running away from!"

Now it's the turn of the police to be lost for words.

Mary continues. "My Dad. I feel a bit sorry for Mum, 'cause she was under his thumb as well, but then she never had the courage to do anything about it, let alone report what was happening to me. He'd got hard up in the seventies, all his own fault, booze, cigarettes and horses, so he gets the idea he's going to rent his daughter out to his mates for a consideration. Mum gets more housekeeping money, so she's alright. Daughter gets more pocket money and can save up for the occasional concert ticket. Problem solved. So you see, I was running *away* from abuse, not towards it."

The bad cop/bad cop facade broken, Jarvis becomes more conciliatory and Roche wisely shuts up altogether.

"So you spent all those years in Formentera?"

"I was there most of the time, yes. I learned the local language, some formal Spanish for all the red tape, and I'm now a Spanish citizen."

"With a Spanish suntan."

"That's just one of the fringe benefits."

"What do you do there?"

"Some bar work. Arts and crafts, it's an industry there for retired hippies. Being English helps, there's plenty of tourists come down on the boat from Ibiza."

"And there's a Mr Terry?"

"Yes, there is, though we never married formally. We decided that wasn't the right direction of travel for either of us."

"What I'd like to do now, with your consent" says Jarvis, "is to get a present day photograph of you and map it on to an older photograph of M...*of yourself*. It'll just be a formality. Comparing bone structure and so forth."

Mary nods.

Sue's in Jarvis' office, discussing developments.

"Yeah, she must have been one mixed up kid", she comments.

"But it looks like life was kind to her in the end. She found a suitable life partner in Mr Terry."

"Mr Terry?"

"I know, that'll make her *Ms* Terry – sounds like a character in some pre-war black and white film."

"Roy Terry's the drummer in the Jim Hellfire Band!" Sue exclaims. Then, after reflection: "Any chance we can book a trip to Formentera?"

"Don't get too excited", says Jarvis. "At that time the age of consent in Spanish territories was only 12. So even if they had a sexual relationship, which they're not going to confess to, we're not going to have anything to do him for. Kidnap's not a possibility because Mary isn't going to say she *was* abducted! It's a sleeping dog we're gonna have to let lie."

"Yeah, and we can't do Daddy anymore, the bastard."

"The cold case perennial", Jarvis agrees.

"Still, at least there won't be any need to get Craig round to perform an ID on her."

"Oh I don't think he'd be of much use there. He won't remember victims, they're just incidentals. It's just his precious squad that he ever cared about."

16

1972

Mary Miles has successfully obtained the autographs of Messrs Franks, Lamotte and Shaw. Graham's also been kind enough to add a personal message – nothing too excessive, just one that acknowledges her first name.

She knows it's going to be tricky getting the signature of Jim Hellfire himself – superstars don't come ten a penny – but she sees his lookalike drummer Roy Terry milling about, and being the person she is, she doesn't want to miss the opportunity.

Roy's happy to provide what she wants, and also to chat for a bit. He notices the other autographs.

"Oh, I see you didn't get the big guy's."

She's a bit overawed, and doesn't know quite what to say. "Is there any chance...?"

"Aw, I'm afraid he's gone, princess. He always makes a run for it before the rest of us."

She looks disappointed.

"I'm sorry," Roy continues, "but you – you need to be getting off home now, don't you?"

"Oh, I'm in no hurry to be getting back there."

"But you'll need to be getting up early in the morning? School and that?"

"To be honest, things aren't that good at home."

"Sorry to hear that. You don't get on with your mum and dad then?"

"It's...it's worse than that."

Now the rocker has a problem. He didn't come out tonight to play the social worker, but he can see and hear the distress in Mary's face and voice.

She tells him a little more.

Now he's stuck. Does he advise going to the police, an action that for him would be counter-intuitive, and which doesn't stand much chance of yielding a desirable outcome anyway?

"Look," he says, "I can protect you for a few hours maybe, but after that – "

Mary is heartened by his interest. "But you're not going out with the band then?"

Roy laughs. "We're not joined at the hip, y'know. They wouldn't even notice me missing. There's a place we can go where you'll be safe for a few hours, away from prying eyes. If anyone does ask, you're my daughter."

She knows she's taking a risk, a big one, but it can't be any worse than going back home – can it?

On the journey he's regaling her with tales of his life in the Balearics. She's impressed.

"It must be great", she says.

"Things could be a lot worse, I agree."

Now for the tricky bit: smuggling someone out of the country. Now it isn't quite so tricky if you are rich and/or have links to organised crime. If both, then bingo. Roy Terry for example is rich enough, he just looks poor, that's rock'n'roll. As for links to organised crime, well who do you think runs the pubs and clubs where every good rocker serves their apprenticeship? That's showbusiness. All it takes now is a couple of phone calls, and there's a private plane waiting at the aerodrome, no problem.

Roy could also, if he wants, arrange for his "connections" to give Mary's dad and his mates a good kicking, but that's hardly peace and love; and besides, Mary herself thinks it'll be far more effective to punish them this way. Bruises heal in time, regrets less so. So the reason for the flight remains on a need-to-know basis.

Doing the wrong thing for the right reasons generates a tremendous buzz among some people. Can anyone honestly sit in judgment over it?

From then on

Mary Miles moves into Roy Terry's home in Formentera. Bit by bit she creates a new existence for herself as "Maria Terry", learns the language, gets a tan, lives platonically with the drummer until they establish a sexual relationship by mutual consent, in keeping with Spanish law.

The relationship is maintained to the present day. Both are happy with it, and with their overall lifestyle. They never marry, but agree they'd be better suited to the equivalent of a common law husband and wife arrangement.

Maria has no objection to her husband going away on tour sometimes, nor to his bringing back the occasional bandmate as a house guest. Nothing untoward happens, as they only have eyes for each other.

The two of them go places together, places of her choosing as much as his; just nowhere in the UK, that's all. There's a whole world out there besides, and they've covered a fair part of it.

However, this ideal situation exists only until Maria Terry gets to hear of the accusations against Jim Hellfire, and decides she needs to act independently to try to make sure the truth comes out. Over and above all else, she needs to make it clear to everyone that she's not his murder victim.

17

Present day

Heather meets Mary in the latter's hotel room. Jarvis has given his blessing to the meeting, hoping that it might lend some clarity to the investigation.

They recognise each other instinctively, and are delighted to meet despite the circumstances.

"You've lost your accent", says Heather on hearing her best friend's voice.

"I've been out of practice for a while", Mary jokes.

Laughter and tears follow for a few minutes before rationality sets in.

"But why didn't you tell me where you were?" asks Heather.

"I know, it was awful and I'm sorry. But it was the only thing I could've done. I couldn't risk my whereabouts becoming general knowledge, so I had to keep it from the good guys as well as the bad."

Mary goes on to recount her tale, starting from the moment they got separated at the concert. She doesn't mince any words about her parents' role in her disappearance.

"Well, I'm glad to see that things worked out so well for you," says Heather, "but something happened to me that night as well."

She gives her personal account of the night's events, something that shocks Mary as she wasn't expecting to hear it this way. "So it was you who made the accusation against Jim?"

"You sound like you don't believe me."

"I'm not saying that."

"I know what happened. It was my body he violated!"

"It's just – "

"Just what?"

"Well when I spoke to Roy that night, he told me that Jim had already left – that's why I couldn't get his autograph."

"And you believed that?"

"Roy's never lied to me", Mary says defensively.

"And did Roy tell you *where* he'd gone?"

"I don't know if he knew for sure. They weren't on each other's case all the time, they weren't like that."

"So he could've been prowling about outside?"

"You don't seriously believe that, do you? A high profile rock star walking the streets looking for jailbait?"

Heather's blood pressure is rising. "I thought you might at least believe me."

"I believe...that what you said happened to you," Mary says with a hesitancy that speaks louder than her actual words, "I just don't believe it's *him*."

"So who was it then?"

"I don't know. I wasn't there. Can *anybody* know after all these years?"

18

"Nice move, sir." On this occasion there was a trace of humour in Sue's sarcasm, which her superior officer managed to register. "Breaking up a young girls' friendship like that."

"Oh, if they'd any sense they'd have raided the mini bar and made it up", Jarvis countered.

"Like a couple of twelve year olds?"

"Well, not twelve year olds with the assistance of a mini bar, I hope."

"McManus says Heather's alright," Sue continues, "but she's not happy with what Mary said to her. Yeah, the drink did calm her down a bit – calmed them both down – but I don't know if it's enough to get them on each other's Christmas card list."

"Well how many of the people you went to school with are still on *your* Christmas card list?"

"Absolutely none! I stopped bothering about the people I went to school with years ago."

"And such is the difference."

"What do you mean?"

"You didn't go to school with anyone who went missing, possibly kidnapped, presumed dead?"

It's a rhetorical question of course, and it's deemed unworthy of a reply.

Jarvis is now fully prepped for giving a psychology tutorial. "We're not talking anything like a normal friendship here. We're talking twelve year old girls in 64 year old women's bodies. Sure, they've got bigger vocabularies and alcohol tolerances, but all the key elements of their lives are frozen in 1972."

Sue's paying attention with an interest she normally lacks on such occasions. "And now they're back together and we find that Mary's been on this big adventure while Heather's been stood stock still."

"Very good point. And what does that tend to provoke in twelve year olds?"

"Jealousy."

"Exactly."

"And the need to make a claim for yourself, to go one better?"

"If you can. It doesn't have to be a positive claim either. You just have to look at those pensioners' clubs where they're always competing to be the sickest person in the group, going about for months on end on crutches that they don't need, reading something about sepsis in the newspaper and making out that they've got it 24 hours later."

"Or making an allegation of rape against Jim Hellfire?"

"Could be."

"But wait a minute...when Heather came to us to tell her story, she'd no idea that Mary was still alive."

"I don't think that's all that important", says Jarvis. "Think about it, at the time the papers and TV news are full of Mary, Mary, Mary – then there's more fuss about her when that record comes out, right? And that subsides, but then come the anniversaries and it's more Mary-ology than the Vatican."

"Well, Heather would have been spoken to by the police at the time as Mary's companion for the evening, wouldn't that have made her feel important?"

"But nowhere near the star of the show. Besides, it would've been a couple of minutes with a uniformed PC at best, down in the notebook as the unimportant comments of a minor. She wasn't talking about the alleged rape then."

"Bottling it up inside her for fifty years."

Jarvis nods.

"So you're coming round to thinking that Hepplewhite might be innocent after all?"

He grins. "I'm not totally convinced, but – "

"You know what the CPS are going to say, though."

"Yeah, and that's why we need to keep pressing."

"But we're running out of things to do the pressing with. We can't keep him in limbo forever."

"We might not have to. Peter Craig was on the blower to me an hour ago, saying that he'd found a couple of photos he thinks might be of interest to us."

Sue sighs. "Oh just by chance, eh? So does that mean we have to roll out the red carpet again?"

"Tomorrow morning, 10:00 hours. Are you sure you can make it?" asks Superintendent Jarvis, looking to see what Sue's reaction will be.

It's a non-verbal one, and he isn't too surprised by it.

19

It's at times like these that Jim Hepplewhite wishes he had the services of a good lapdog again. The birdwatching has been an education, a valuable use of his time and even a small contribution to his bank balance, but in the end, because of their physical separation, birds don't provide the two-way emotional involvement that the right breed of dog can.

This afternoon he has instead the pleasure of his local church minister at home. Now sherry with the rector isn't exactly rock'n'roll, even by millennial standards, but Jim isn't bothered too much by that. Someone with a listening ear is a definite improvement on watching the telly or thinking of something to do on the internet or hearing the absence of his songs on Responsible Rock Radio.

The man of the cloth has left it a respectable amount of time before deciding to contact Jim and arrange this visit. He doesn't want to be seen offending anybody but, knowing that there are two sides to every story, and keeping in mind the fact that Jim's been an enthusiastic and generous supporter of the church in recent years, he'd be failing in his duty not to offer him the courtesy of his presence.

"I've never been inside the castle before", he declares.

"I know," says Jim, "perhaps I should've been more hospitable in the past."

"Well, you're a busy man."

"Not quite as busy at the moment. Still, I expect your predecessors paid a few visits in the old days."'

The rector grins. "It might have depended on whose side they were on. Civil War, I mean."

"Yeah, well, this has been all about taking sides, it seems to me."

"I don't – "

"You've got to believe me, I didn't do the things they're accusing me of. I know I got up to things when I was younger that were bloody stupid, and I've put my hands up to them."

"And you've been forgiven for them, have no doubt about that."

"But this...having my home invaded by these goons, then having the grounds excavated, having my dogs dug up because they think it might be a missing girl, it just makes me wanna explode."

"Well I've never been in that sort of situation myself, though as a church minister I've had colleagues who came under suspicion – sometimes rightly, often times maliciously."

"Yes, you're not in a good position, are you?" Jim concedes. "Your business is to help and inspire, to save souls, not to have your own actions and motives questioned."

"There's a *little* bit of similarity in our chosen professions, then."

Jim manages a genuine smile, a rare thing in recent days.

"I think we need to pray", says the rector. "Pray for yourself of course, but pray that justice prevails. He is a God of justice, after all. And, though you might not feel too much like it at the moment, pray for your accuser and the police that they find their way to the truth."

"Okay. I'm happy to do that."

They conclude the meeting in prayer.

20

Sue wakes with an annoying bout of nausea. The thought of meeting Craig again might be seen as a contributing factor, but more likely it's a side effect of a new prescription of Big Pharma poison that the GP has courteously provided.

She wishes she hadn't bothered with that appointment. It's the old merry-go-round: you complain of diarrhoea and they give you something that causes constipation.

She thinks about pulling a sickie, but decides instead to hold it in abeyance until this case is satisfactorily resolved. She's got too much at stake with this one and, though she's never really been a perfectionist, she decides she should make the effort.

All she can face for breakfast is a couple of Rich Tea biscuits and a weak tea with sugar. She hopes Craig won't make her feel any more sick.

The old man is already comfortably installed in Jarvis' office when Sue joins the party. She nods to her superior.

"Sir. *Mister* Craig", she says almost dismissively.

Craig doesn't offer a greeting of his own. "You tried the drugs approach with Hepplewhite, like I said?"

"It didn't lead us anywhere."

"No?"

She puts on her best mocking cool-dude accent. "'Hey man, look, I was so stoned out of my mind that I didn't know what I was doing. So I must have done it, yeah.' It's not something you can easily convert into a signed confession."

"So now it's *your* turn to be getting nowhere?"

Jarvis intervenes. "Not so, Peter. We've made some very significant steps forward. I can tell you for instance, though we'd appreciate your keeping quiet about it for the time being, that we've managed to locate Mary Miles."

Craig looks amazed. "What? Well, where's she buried then? Somewhere round here?"

Sue has to steal a point. "She isn't buried anywhere. She's alive and well and staying in a city centre hotel."

"I don't believe it...which hotel?"

"Now you know we can't tell you that", says Jarvis. "We're having a media blackout at least pro tem. There's some sensitive information relating to both her disappearance and reappearance, and we need to be sure about the legal aspects before we start grandstanding about it."

"I should think there *should* be", says Craig. "You *are* convinced it really is Mary Miles?"

"Her best friend, the girl she went to the concert with, is convinced that it's her", says Sue.

"Hang on," says Craig, "this isn't some little game they dreamt up in the playground, is it? 'Let's make fools of the police for 50 years'?"

"And why would they want to do that?" asks Sue, raising her voice.

"Oh well, like I said last time, getting themselves brainwashed by these ragamuffins."

"So it's all one big conspiracy then? You weren't saying *that* last time when you were going to string up Jim Hellfire and anybody who had anything remotely to do with him."

Jarvis plays the voice of reason again. "The murder investigation's over, but the rape investigation's still live. Mary's friend still says she was sexually assaulted after the concert."

"Well what do you want me to do about that?" says Craig.

Sue reminds him of the purpose of his second visit. "You said you had photos you wanted

"I'm not sure if they're relevant anymore."

"We'd be grateful if you'd let us be the judges of that", says Jarvis.

"Very well." Craig has an old briefcase leaning against the chair he's sat in. He takes out a couple of photographs. One is a group photo of a bunch of young bobbies, Class of '69 or whenever. "Pictures I found of Alan Rogers."

He's barely identifiable in the large group, and was probably never meant to be – it's one of those things you hang up somewhere at the station until a new cohort comes along. Craig thinks Rogers is third from the left on the front row, but there's a physical similarity about many of the subjects, as tended to be the case in those days.

"I don't think this is going to be a lot of use, Peter", says Jarvis apologetically.

"I do have one other of Rogers alone", Peter replies, and shows them the other photo. This one's much clearer: a head and shoulders shot of a quite handsome and smart young man in his twenties, dressed in a plain clothes jacket, collar length hair, regulation issue police moustache ("which came and went", according to Craig).

It's enough to generate interest on Sue's part. She looks meaningfully at Jarvis.

"I think we might need to keep hold of this one", the boss announces.

"That was taken about the time of the Miles case", says Craig.

"He'd already be married with children by that point?" asks Jarvis.

Craig nods, then continues: "Bit of a tragedy there, if I remember rightly. Son had one of these inherited medical conditions, had to keep him wrapped in cotton wool."

"What, you mean like cystic fibrosis?"

"Couldn't tell you. I'm not a doctor, am I? Does it matter?"

"No, probably not", admits Jarvis.

21

1972

Bootle Street police station is a stone's throw from the Free Trade Hall, Manchester's premier music venue. It's common for police officers, sometimes showing out in uniform, sometimes in civvies, to be amongst the crowd to prevent trouble.

The genre of music for the night is the determinant of the police response. If the Hallé are in residence, for example, there's no real need for any officers to become involved unless it's to stop any post-concert disputes about taxis back to Cheshire from Albert Square getting out of hand.

If it's a less formal type of music, then the police presence needs to be adjusted to fit. Screaming pop fans pulling each other's hair and fainting all over the place needs to be dealt with one way – call it damage limitation – while the more intellectually demanding groups demand not only some drug awareness ("intent to supply" is a popular offence on such occasions) but also alertness to the possibilities for civil disobedience, especially when the performers on stage have a reputation as political animals, eager to get a crowd of potential young Bolsheviks on the march, daubing graffiti on the walls and throwing up on the pavement. It was thought to be a good idea among the senior officers at Bootle Street to have a few plain clothes detectives, if they looked the part, the gig, and to call for backup if the situation warranted it.

Detective Constable Alan Rogers was an obvious choice for such a role, and he's conducted it with apparent ease and skill on numerous previous occasions. He'd be well at home with the Jim Hellfire Band concert tonight; why, he even likes a few of Hellfire's songs, so he can let himself go if he chooses without looking stupid.

He sits back and enjoys the concert, although he's a bit more enthusiastic about the support band than most of the audience. There's no real trouble before or after the event, just the expected bustle, but nothing that even the most puritanical defender of the peace would wish to categorise as a criminal offence.

He lets the crowd disperse to whatever paths they've chosen – typically the boozer or the bus – and begins his stroll around the outside of the building, a "just in case" protocol he feels it necessary to follow. Plenty of litter of course, which is a disgrace but what can you do if you haven't seen who dropped it, but nothing valuable or incriminating among it.

He sees a girl ahead of him, looking around indecisively. She keeps her back to him, and he quickens his pace until he's right behind her. He puts his hand on her shoulder, and puts on what he imagines is a cool rock star voice.

"You looking for somebody?"

She turns round and sees a cool rock star. She doesn't know what to say.

"Umm...my...my friend", she eventually blurts out.

"Looks like they've abandoned you", says the cool rock star. "Will I do instead?"

She's nervous. But before she's had time to think, he's got hold of her. He pushes her against a wall, not harshly enough to cause injury but enough to disorient her as he takes out a syringe and a bottle of Actrapid insulin, prescribed for his young son, that he keeps in his inside jacket pocket for moments like this. He quickly draws up a sufficient dose and injects it into the girl's upper arm. She offers little physical resistance, and he's able to cover her mouth once he's pocketed the medication, so all he needs to do now is wait for it to take effect so he can perform a sex act on her.

That done, he slips a £5 note in her bag and walks her to an all night café, making as if he's escorting a drunk, a talent he perfected in his uniform days. He sits her at a table away from the windows, gets a coffee for himself and a large Coke for her, which he has to help her drink, at least for the first few tastes.

"You really need to drink this", he says, more for the benefit of the handful of other customers than for his companion's.

He re-orders the same drinks for both of them. She starts to sober up.

"What bus are you on?" he asks her.

She tries to think. "Err...the 50? Yeah, the 50, that's right."

"Then I'll walk you to the night bus stop when you've finished that", he says, indicating her drink. "You make sure you get off at the right stop."

Heather Williamson becomes more aware of her surroundings as the bus plods along Kingsway. A couple of stops from now is where she needs to get off. She anticipates a row with her parents, and wonders where the last few hours could have gone.

She gets off at the right stop, but only just.

1974

Alan Rogers leaves the police force, and within a short while begins a new job as a swimming instructor. His first posts are at swimming baths in North Manchester, but after a few summers he's working at Burton Road and High Street, which are much more convenient for home. He continues to abuse children for as long as the urge remains in him, the victims are docile, and the investigative techniques poor.

2007

Alan Rogers is awarded the title of Member of the Most Excellent Order of the British Empire for his 30+ years of service in helping young people learn to swim.

2008

Alan Rogers dies.

22

Present day

McManus shows Heather the close up shot of Alan Rogers. The sight of it startles her a bit.

"Do you recognise this guy?" he asks.

She's uneasy. "I, um, I don't know. The moustache –"

The moustache that came and went according to requirements.

"Do you want to see it without the moustache?"

Heather nods. This isn't a videofit so McManus, ever obliging, cuts a thin strip of plain paper and covers the problematic item. It isn't art, but it's enough for her.

"That's the man who attacked me!"

"You sure about that?"

"Yeah. But it's not – "

"It's not what?"

"It's not Jim Hellfire."

"Thanks. I needed you to say that yourself."

"So who is he?" she asks. Now the implications are coming together in her head, she's starting to feel guilty.

"A man named Alan Rogers. He was a swimming instructor." He decides not to declare Rogers' police role.

"Was? You mean he's dead?"

McManus nods.

"Well I can hardly say I'm sorry."

There were different levels of resemblance to guitar heroes. You could affect the facial expressions, the manner of dress and the swagger maybe, but if you weren't blessed with the same facial features the similarity could only ever be superficial. You could arrange your hair or wear an approved hat for the gig, but tomorrow morning you'd be back in your trilby and raincoat for the day job. But if you bore a facial similarity, you could put on the T shirt and jeans of your choice and still be mistaken for the genuine article, as was the case here.

"You sure she didn't just recognise him from the baths?" Sue asks.

"Positive, ma'am", says McManus. "By the time that Rogers was working as a swimming instructor, he was in different districts of Manchester to the ones that Heather was ever likely to visit. Besides, at her school swimming was made an option for games lessons at age 14 – they probably expected you to have learned by then – and she never exercised the option. She'd maybe go to the Galleon once or twice with friends, but Rogers had nothing to do with that place, at least not professionally."

"Yeah, it makes their meeting up in other circumstances unlikely."

"He'd be just another Seventies guy with a 'tache, even if she did see him in the shops."

"I'm interested in knowing more about Alan Rogers' death", says Sue.

"Ahead of you there, ma'am. Heart attack. Dead on arrival at MRI 29 February 2008, Leap Year Day. Didn't get to snuggle up to his MBE for too long."

"He'd only have been about sixty. He clearly kept himself fit, and he was the athletic type. Plus, health monitoring is so much better in the 21st century. Bit unusual, don't you think?"

"What, do you suspect anything?"

"Just thinking out loud. There are ways you could induce, engineer cardiac arrest if you wanted to."

McManus is intrigued by this line of thinking. "You got anybody in mind for this?"

Sue doesn't beat about the bush this time. "The widow?"

"She won't be able to tell us anything now. She died herself last year."

"You are so thorough, Jack! Do you know anything about the son, the one who had to be wrapped in cotton wool according to Peter Craig? Is he still with us?"

"Alive and well and making a fortune in Seattle. IT genius, two or three rungs above my level, Name of Matthew Rogers, active on Facebook and all the rest, a bit too active for my liking. All checks out though, born Manchester, United Kingdom, educated Cambridge University, it's one of the few Anglo-American profiles that *are* believable. Only likely to come to this country for conferences, weddings and funerals."

"Oh, well perhaps it might have been some poor kid he abused at the baths, then. People can nurse grudges for a very long time. The MBE must've been the final insult."

"If indeed it was a murder at all."

"Indeed", Sue sighs. "We may never know or care."

"Do you want to give Jim Hepplewhite the good news?" asks Jarvis. "You being such a fan?"

"I'd rather not", says Sue. "I don't think he was too impressed with me when we met. Wouldn't it look better coming from someone of higher authority?"

"I don't think matters of police hierarchy are of much concern to folks like our James. But if it gets you off the hook –"

23

"Totem Pole Dance", an instrumental from the live album, is playing in Sue's head as she's waiting for the debriefing to start. Credited exclusively to J. Hellfire, but owing more than a little to The Shadows and Duane Eddy – but you could package anything you liked up in '72 and the fans would regard it as new music – it was played as part of the Instrumental Feature one of the rock radio stations last night. Suddenly it's safe to listen to Jim Hellfire's music again.

The chords are still echoing as the meeting gets under way. Sue has a habit of switching off at these times when she's waiting to speak: her superiors just indulge in a predictable cliché-fest – Bullshit Bingo cards at the ready, everybody – and the lower ranking officers relate their experiences using all the right expressions, never wanting to rock the boat. The right boxes are ticked, but there's no real enlightenment; it's paper clip pushing, civil service style.

Eventually it's Sue's turn. She gets up briskly. "Look, I know it's a bit of a disappointment to some of us that we haven't been able to charge anybody in connection with this, but unfortunately it's a bit difficult to arrest and charge dead people." It isn't intended as a humorous remark, and it certainly isn't treated as one. "Victims like to see justice done, don't they? But look at it this way: we've resolved a case that nobody else has been able to, and we've granted the people who matter some closure, so hopefully they can get on with what's left of their lives."

She pauses, but remains standing. Murmurs among the audience indicate that there's a "But" coming on.

Sue anticipates this. "*And*", she stresses, "I'd like to add one thing more. The people responsible for the sexual abuse here were heads of families, outwardly respectable people, not your sad solitary single nonces. Let that be a warning to you if you're tempted to fall into the old stereotypes. Do that and you just turn into another Peter Craig, fifty years out of date. And that's not the direction we should be travelling." Sentiments in fact transposed from her recent woke conference to this present situation, but she doesn't mind if the cap fits.

Jarvis takes Sue aside afterwards. "I was very interested to hear your experiences. Very thought-provoking."

"Well I try to tell it as I find it, sir."

"Yes, I don't think there's any arguing with that. But you may've been a bit unfair. It was Peter Craig and his photograph that finally managed to solve the case."

"Yes, after we'd done all the hard work. Is that all, sir?"

"How'd you fancy a fish and chip lunch?"

"Beg pardon?"

"The investigation's over, it's time to wind down. My treat."

"Well...I haven't been feeling too good lately."

"Yes, they were saying that you haven't been playing your normal part in the canteen culture these past few days. You all right? Eaten anything you shouldn't have?"

"I don't think it's anything like that."

Jarvis knows he's getting nowhere, so he changes the subject back. "It's a licensed fish restaurant."

"Well maybe just a small portion..."

24

Jim offers a prayer of thanksgiving. He's now back as a church regular, heartened by the quick positive outcome of his recent meeting with the rector. Other folk might explain the turn of events differently, but that's their business. He gives short shrift to those who fell for all the tabloid and telly twaddle, the "no smoke without fire" platoon. It's not an ideal position for a Christian to be in, but he shouldn't be the one to have to go around making apologies.

He's invited the surviving JHB members, Roy Terry, Graham Shaw and their partners round to a small celebration at the castle. He announces that his plans for the future might include a gospel album, to which both musicians are invited to contribute; bass, keyboard and all the trimmings duties to be allocated in due course.

"You sure about this, Jim?" says Roy. "It's all a bit Cliff, isn't it?"

"Come on, man," Graham offers, "have you forgotten all those riffs we borrowed from The Shadows?"

"'Good artists borrow, great artists steal'" says Jim. "I freely admit I stole from everybody I could, and I'd like five million other offences to be taken into consideration." Laughter ensues. "But now I think is the time to pay something back."

"But don't you think you need to ditch the Hellfire tag if you're gonna do a gospel LP?" Roy asks quite sensibly. "Not really befitting, is it?"

Jim grins. "I hadn't really thought about that. But one of the themes of the record could be that nobody's beyond redemption."

"Well it beats playing the irony card, like the snowflakes do", says Graham.

"Oh there's nothing ironic about it, Gray."

Conversation inevitably gets round to Jim's adversities of recent times.

"How did you keep your head, man?" asks Roy.

"Well, knowing I was innocent helped. Even when everybody else seemed to be thinking I was guilty."

"Hey, we never –" Roy and Graham are almost in chorus.

"I don't mean you guys. I mean those in authority, and the dudes on the streets who believe everything they're told."

"The cops, they treated you badly?" asks Graham.

"Well, like you'd expect cops to. Tell you what, though, that Chief Inspector wasn't a bad looker for an old 'un."

"What, you mean if the circumstances had been different you might've - ?"

Jim smiles again. "Oh, it never would've worked. I can't imagine anyone as buttoned-up as her being into our music. Y'know, she didn't even bother to call me up once they knew they had nothing to charge me with. Got some bullshit artist called Jarvis to do the job instead."

Heather and Mary are picking up the pieces. They're both survivors of child abuse at the end of the day, though the scenarios were different, and they've come to realise that. This isn't some sisterhood of sadness, however, nor a man-hating enterprise – Mary can testify to the fact that some men at least are trustworthy and can have an affirmative impact – and they're seeking to conduct their future friendship along such lines. Mary, predictably, is taking the lead here, and agrees with Roy that the first thing they can do is invite Heather to spend some time on the island with them. They'll play it by ear, they resolve, and do things by consensus.

Heather's started listening to her favourite bands from her teenage years. She's wishing now that she hadn't flogged that JHB vinyl to her schoolmate – it must be worth a fortune now, and there weren't any leaps or scratches on the discs when she got rid of them. But she's making do with YouTube, and she might keep her eyes peeled for a cheap CD or two.

A heavily redacted version of Heather and Mary's stories is finally made available for media speculators. They're not doing interviews, even if Oprah comes hunting with a chequebook. If they do get to write a book about it, they'll do so on their own terms, okay?

No-one has been brought to book over offences committed against Mary Miles in the early seventies. No death bed confessions from weary old men; but then, given the likely "client" profiles of alcohol- and high tar tobacco-dependent working class dimwits, there's not much chance that any of them got to be old men anyway.

Eric Tallis is excited. As excited as a 67-year-old male has any right to be. The coffee dates with his sister-in-law have turned out well, and he's seriously considering moving up to a more advanced level. There's no chance of "musical differences" coming in to spoil the party like they did so frequently in the seventies.

Sue Tallis really doesn't want to know. She's trying hard not to form a mental picture of their association and, though she feels she could invoke a number of Biblical imperatives regarding responsibilities towards your brother's widow, she decides not to.

She's round at Eric's place for a cuppa and a chat. After giving her round-up of her role in resolving the Jim Hellfire case, she allows matters to get back to a more personal level.

"So will I need to change my name to Tallis-Tallis?" she asks without noticeable expression.

"Oh, you mean like Jeffrey Hammond-Hammond of Jethro Tull?"

"If you say so."

"Well, I suppose that's up to you." He carries on with mock seriousness: "But I don't want any lectures about treating your mother right. I knew her before you did, don't forget. I reckon I know how to please her."

"Spare me the details, uncle, please. You can have my blessing. Do as you will, I'm off to watch some cricket."

"What, in this weather?"

"In Cape Town."

"Well, mind how you go then."

"You what?"

Eric smirks. "World murder capital, isn't it?"

CROSS THEIR NAME OUT

A DCI Tallis: Celebrity Crimewave short story

It was getting on Sue Tallis' nerves that a lot of the cases being referred to the Celebrity Task Force didn't actually involve genuine celebrities at all. Reality show contestants, YouTube bores, influencers, kebab shop owners who became TikTok sensations...even the Warhol definition of fame was stretching it a bit for no-marks like these.

To be honest, she'd been irritable since her return from her break in South Africa. Another holiday romance that wasn't. She had received some consolation for the double failure one of her favourite cricketers on their international debut from the chappie sat next to her in the crowd, who let out an impressive list of players who'd failed in their first test match but gone on to have remarkable careers: Jacques Kallis, Hashim Amla, Graham Gooch, Viv Richards, even Don Bradman.

Sue's one of those many cricket followers who take an interest in stats, but this guy was bordering on the obsessive. "Cricket is the perfect marriage of maths and physics", he said spontaneously on Day 3. Now who in their right mind would say things like that, off the cuff?

She put up with it all though: he was well-mannered and articulate, if not much of a listener, and he didn't look her in the eye all that much. Above all, he was a bit of a looker, maybe not the best-groomed bloke she'd ever encountered but with the right clothes and body spray...he was about her age, which was good. She thought he'd develop a taste for her attempts at Yorkshire puddings with time.

She gave him her email, and he promised to contact her when she got home, but he never did. She never bothered to take any of his details, which might have been a mistake – a Delivery Failure Notice waiting to happen?

And suppose things *had* worked out? Were regular revisits to Cape Town a realistic possibility?

All this of course was fallout from her mother's more modest but apparently more productive adventure in the romance department. But they wanted companionship in old age, not sex, surely? Sue dismissed all thoughts of a same-surname Norfolk wedding, it was nothing like that, it just rankled a little.

Now for this rubbish case. It was one for a DS, perhaps accompanied by a raw but enthusiastic Detective Constable, not a DCI. Roche, who was getting lazier by the minute, Sue felt, could have taken the lead, but as it happened this was his week for a holiday.

So Sue was left grumbling all the way to Bimbo College Bolton, as the wits of CTF would have it: get your degree in Hair Nails & Beauty and stay on to do a Master's in skateboarding. A local meat and two veg cook – calling her a chef was pure hype – who'd blagged her way on to *Saturday*

Kitchen one week when all the regulars were on tour, had collapsed in unexplained circumstances on the premises. But she wasn't even dead, just on a life support machine: even less reason to call a senior officer out.

Her name is Bella Groome. Her one TV appearance to date was surrounded by all the expected local newspaper fuss-about-nothing, and was quickly followed by an invitation to an honorary lectureship at the seat of knowledge, despite her having no academic qualifications, with the specific aim of encouraging the creation of employment in the community, particularly among under-represented groups. The end result, it almost goes without saying, was army of minimum wage youth selling overpriced ready meals that you could cook yourself for about 10p per person.

The Peter Kay Lecture Theatre was regularly packed, with curiosity-seekers as well as regular students, and – wonder of wonders – it raised the university's profile! The admin bosses couldn't be happier.

So why should anyone want to ruin things?

Sue started on familiar territory. "Did she have any allergies?"

"Not to our knowledge", said the CEO's secretary, an overweight tattooed slob who was probably ten years younger than she looked. She got Bella's details up on screen and scanned them for a few milliseconds. "No."

"No history of diabetes or epilepsy?"

"We went through that with the paramedics. No."

"She's not vegetarian or vegan? It can make you ill, eating what you're not supposed to -"

"You gotta be joking. Have you seen what she puts in her recipes? More fat and gristle than a pound shop."

"What, you didn't like her recipes?"

"No, I love 'em – look at me."

"Well did you know of anyone here expressing a dislike for her food? Or for *her*?"

"We don't have things like that on our records."

"Never mind the records. You people are supposed to know everything about the subculture of the organisation, all the bitching and in-fighting that doesn't make it to the press releases."

"In that case I think what you said applies to about 99% of people with anything to do with the university."

Bella's students weren't much better. Nutritionists who thought vegans could eat honey because all you had to do to obtain it was drill a hole in a honey tree, that "vegan" was just a sub-literate way of shorthanding the word "vegetarian". Half of them don't even know their proteins from their carbs; what it is to be young.

"What exactly went on here today?" Sue asked a group of them, all staring at each other for suggestions for possible responses.

After a while, one of the males replied: "It was a bake-in."

"And that involved...?"

"Making bread and cakes for Bella", said one of the bimbos.

"And her tasting them?" What Sue really wanted to say was "do they really give you degrees for that".

The girl nodded.

"Ah, now we're getting somewhere. And you all contributed to this effort?"

A general murmur indicating "yes".

"And it was just you twelve?"

Response as above.

"Then one of you is a poisoner. Any confessions or do I have to get the heavy mob in to organise things?"

For a breach of Health & Safety regulations, Mohammed Iqbal was sent down with immediate effect; nothing of course compared to the lengthy prison sentence he got for attempted murder. The university, in addition to a heavy fine, was docked 100 points in the Fifth Division of the League of Former Polytechnics and Modern Day Opportunists, seriously damaging its ability to entice cash cow foreign students and give a lifeline to the surrounding ghost town.

Iqbal, it turned out, was simply in a fit of pique about the one star hygiene rating given to his family's takeaway not far from the university. The prophet was not cited in his defence.

Bella Groome made a full recovery, and his on TV and the usual media channels as frequently and annoyingly as possible. Sue left a Get Well

Soon card by the side of her bed when Bella was too ill to talk, for no good reason.

"So you see," said Jarvis to Sue post hoc, "you were the perfect person for the job after all, with your extensive knowledge of foodstuffs and the like, we haven't got any DSs who can match you there."

"Fine," she said with a smile, "so why do I feel like Poirot?"

Printed in Great Britain
by Amazon

39674538R00081